Dear Parents:

Congratulations! Your child is taking the first steps on an exciting journey. The destination? Independent reading!

STEP INTO READING® will help your child get there. The program offers five steps to reading success. Each step includes fun stories and colorful art or photographs. In addition to original fiction and books with favorite characters, there are Step into Reading Non-Fiction Readers, Phonics Readers and Boxed Sets, Sticker Readers, and Comic Readers—a complete literacy program with something to interest every child.

Learning to Read, Step by Step!

Ready to Read   Preschool–Kindergarten
• big type and easy words • rhyme and rhythm • picture clues
For children who know the alphabet and are eager to begin reading.

Reading with Help   Preschool–Grade 1
• basic vocabulary • short sentences • simple stories
For children who recognize familiar words and sound out new words with help.

Reading on Your Own   Grades 1–3
• engaging characters • easy-to-follow plots • popular topics
For children who are ready to read on their own.

Reading Paragraphs   Grades 2–3
• challenging vocabulary • short paragraphs • exciting stories
For newly independent readers who read simple sentences with confidence.

Ready for Chapters   Grades 2–4
• chapters • longer paragraphs • full-color art
For children who want to take the plunge into chapter books but still like colorful pictures.

STEP INTO READING® is designed to give every child a successful reading experience. The grade levels are only guides; children will progress through the steps at their own speed, developing confidence in their reading. The F&P Text Level on the back cover serves as another tool to help you choose the right book for your child.

Remember, a lifetime love of reading starts with a single step!

For Bill and Phyllis

Library of Congress Cataloging-in-Publication Data is available upon request.
ISBN 978-0-593-43228-0 (trade) — ISBN 978-0-593-43229-7 (lib. bdg.)

Printed in the United States of America
10 9 8 7 6 5 4 3 2 1

This book has been officially leveled by using the F&P Text Level Gradient™ Leveling System.

world of
ERIC CARLE
The Very
Busy Spider

by Eric Carle

Random House New York

Early one morning, the wind blew
a spider across the field.
A thin, silky thread trailed from
her body.

The spider landed on a fence post near a farmyard and began to spin a web with her silky thread.

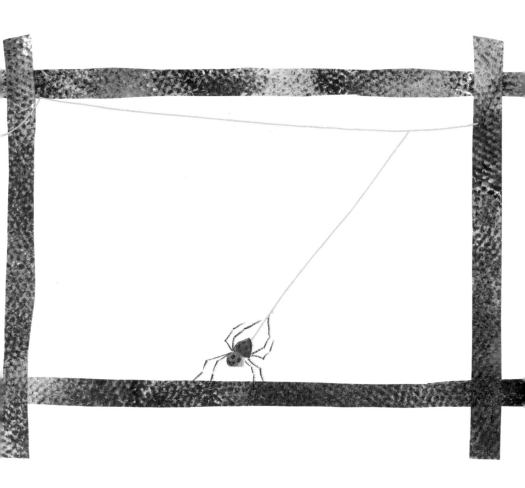

"Neigh! Neigh!" said the horse.

"Want to go for a ride?"

The spider didn't answer.

She was very busy spinning her web.

"Moo! Moo!" said the cow.

"Want to eat some grass?"

The spider didn't answer.

She was very busy spinning her web.

"Bah! Bah!" bleated the sheep.

"Want to run in the meadow?"

The spider didn't answer.

She was very busy spinning her web.

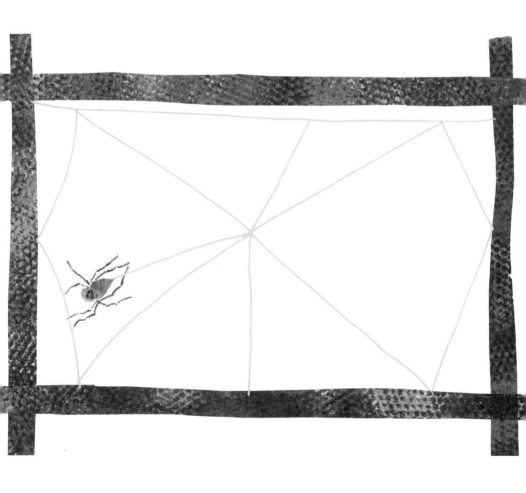

"Maa! Maa!" said the goat.

"Want to jump on the rocks?"

The spider didn't answer.

She was very busy spinning her web.

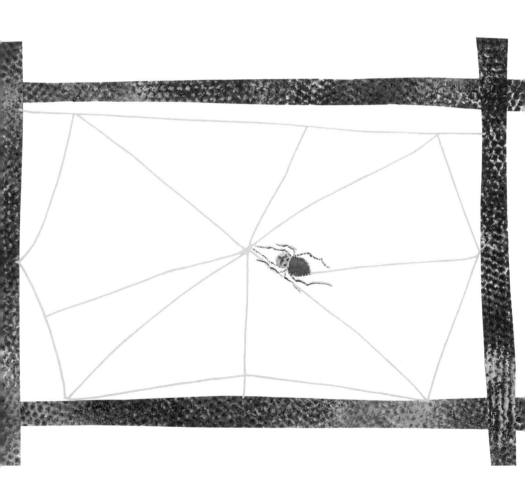

"Oink! Oink!" grunted the pig.

"Want to roll in the mud?"

The spider didn't answer.

She was very busy spinning her web.

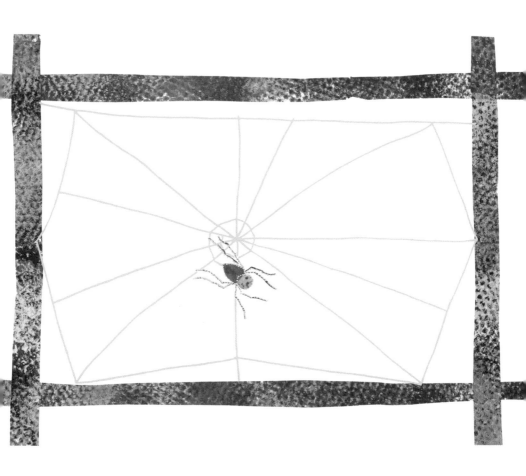

"Woof! Woof!" barked the dog.

"Want to chase a cat?"

The spider didn't answer.

She was very busy spinning her web.

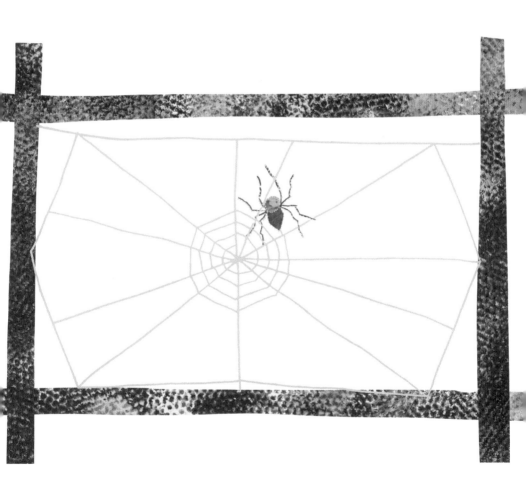

"Meow! Meow!" cried the cat.

"Want to take a nap?"

The spider didn't answer.

She was very busy spinning her web.

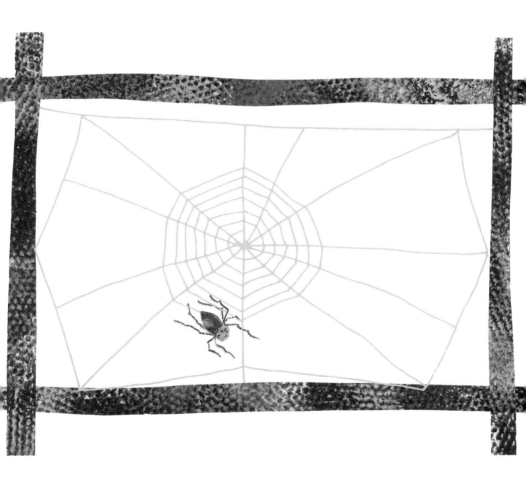

"Quack! Quack!" called the duck.

"Want to go for a swim?"

The spider didn't answer.

She had now finished her web.

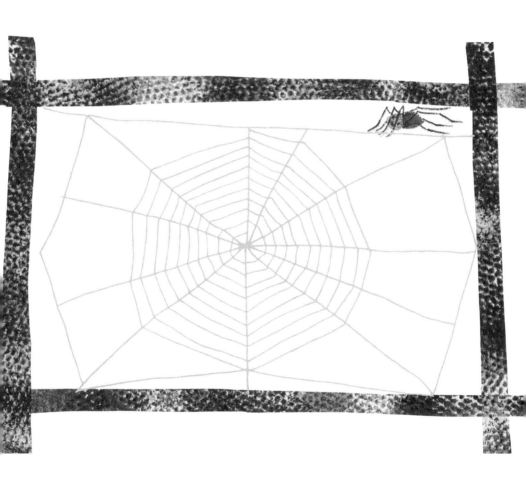

"Cock-a-doodle-do!"

crowed the rooster.

"Want to catch a pesty fly?"

And the spider caught the fly in
her web . . . just like that!

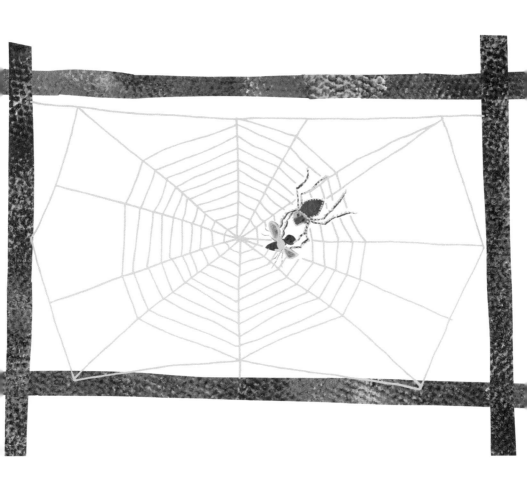

"Whoo? Whoo?" asked the owl.

"Who built this beautiful web?"

The spider didn't answer.

She had fallen asleep.

It had been a very, very busy day.